Marooned
in Fraggle Rock

By David Young
Pictures by Barbara McClintock

Muppet Press
Holt, Rinehart and Winston
NEW YORK

Published by Holt, Rinehart and Winston,
383 Madison Avenue, New York, New York 10017.

Library of Congress Cataloging in Publication Data
Young, David.
Marooned in Fraggle Rock.
Summary: The big birthday party for Boober is
shockingly held up when he and Red are trapped in a cave-in.
[1. Birthdays—Fiction.   2. Caves—Fiction.
3. Puppets—Fiction]   I. McClintock, Barbara, ill.   II. Title.
PZ7.Y853Mar   1984   [E]   84-6670

ISBN: 0-03-000719-4
First Edition

Printed in the United States of America
1 3 5 7 9 10 8 6 4 2

ISBN 0-03-000719-4

Contents

I

A Party for Boober

IT was a great day for a party in Fraggle Rock!

Now, as any of the Fraggles will tell you (and they will if you give them half a chance), *any* day is a great day for a party in Fraggle Rock. That's because the Fraggles like nothing better than having fun, and you can have lots and lots of fun at a party. Of course you can also have a huge amount of fun swimming in the pool in the Great Hall, at the center of the Rock. And you can have *tons* of fun playing Jump the Bump and Bag the Fraggle and all the other games that the Fraggles have invented. Fraggles only work for thirty minutes a week, you see, so they have plenty of time to do all sorts of wonderfully fun things.

But a party certainly provides you with a delightful reason to have as much fun as you possibly can.

This party was a special one, for it was Boober's surprise birthday party. Gobo, Wembley, Red, and Mokey were Boober's best friends, and they had planned the whole thing. They really wanted Boober to enjoy himself, because he usually didn't. Boober was a very un-Fragglish Fraggle. He *hated* parties, good cheer, high spirits, and fun in general. He never played games and always complained about everything. As a matter of fact, Boober was just about the gloomiest Fraggle you could possibly imagine.

Boober worried all the time. He worried while he was doing the laundry, which was his job in Fraggle Rock. He worried while he was eating breakfast, lunch, and dinner, and while he was having his midnight radish (radishes are the Fraggles' favorite food). He worried so much that his four friends suspected that he really must love worrying. (And although Boober would never admit it, it was just a little bit true.)

But even though Boober was not a fan of birthdays and parties, his friends were determined to make this party a roaring success.

Gobo was standing in the middle of the Great Hall, busy stirring up the refreshments—a delicious pot of lima bean soup. Wembley, who was Gobo's roommate, was standing around trying to be helpful. Other Fraggles crisscrossed back and forth across the Hall, stringing up colored rolls of something that looked like crepe paper but was really dried cave moss. The Hall was beginning to look very festive indeed.

Wembley hovered over Gobo, who was stirring away with a long wooden spoon. The soup bubbled merrily in its huge cooking pot. Gobo frowned.

"Can I have a taste?" Wembley asked. "Can I, Gobo?"

Gobo frowned some more. "Sure, for what it's worth," he said. He offered the steaming spoon to Wembley, who sniffed it and then took a little sip.

"You know what, Gobo? This lima bean soup is missing something."

"What's that?"

"Lima beans!" Wembley laughed.

Now, Gobo was a brave and fearless Fraggle, and a natural leader. He was also cheerful and good-natured, and no Fraggle could accuse him of lacking a sense of humor. But right now he was not in the mood for jokes.

"I wonder where Red is," Gobo grumbled. "She was supposed to bring back those lima beans *ages* ago. I'll never get this soup ready in time for the party. Do me a favor, Wembley—would you head over to the Pantry and find Red and the lima beans?"

"Okay," Wembley said agreeably, heading off at a trot. Wembley was extremely agreeable. In fact he always agreed with everyone about everything.

"And bring Mokey back with you!" Gobo called after him. "She's the only one who knows how to season this stuff just the way Boober likes it!"

Wembley nodded over his shoulder and kept on going. As he trotted along through the caves and tunnels of Fraggle Rock, he hummed a little tune. This was going to be a wonderful day. Boober's party and lima bean soup and all his friends together. It would be *perfect!*

The underground caverns of Fraggle Rock twisted and turned and went every which way and then back again. Wembley trotted up one tunnel and down another, still humming. The caves of the Rock were filled with warm, glowing colors and fascinating rock formations. And there little hollows everywhere—perfect for exploring, or hiding in when you played Find the Fraggle.

Wembley made a right turn and then a left and then another left, and then he was at the Pantry—the place where all the Fraggle food was stored. Happily, Mokey was sitting right outside on a ledge, with her diary and pencil in hand. She looked thoughtful.

"Hi, Mokey!" said Wembley, waving his tail in greeting.

"Oh, hello, Wembley! I was just composing a little poem in honor of Boober's birthday. Would you like to hear it?"

"Sure!" Wembley was thrilled. It was a real honor to be the first Fraggle to hear one of Mokey's poems. Mokey was a very sensitive and artistic Fraggle. She was always writing poetry or drawing pictures, and all the Fraggles admired her very much.

Mokey cleared her throat and began:

> "Hail to thee, oh Boober,
>   On this, your natal day.
>   You conjure up the whitest wash
>   From clothes of dingy gray.
>   We wish you happy birthday
>   And many happy more.
>   And hope you'll soon be happier
>   Than you have been before."

"Gosh, that's wonderful, Mokey! And speaking of Boober's birthday, I'm looking for Red. Gobo sent me to find her. She was supposed to bring the lima beans to the Great Hall. Oh, and Gobo wanted you, too... to help season the soup."

"Red's inside," Mokey said, hopping off her ledge. "Come on, Wembley. We'll find her together."

Red was Mokey's best friend, but she and Mokey weren't a

bit alike. Where Mokey was gentle and sensitive, Red was out-
going and energetic. She was a daring sports Fraggle, and her
dives into the pool in the Great Hall were the envy of all. She
was always running around and *doing* things. Wembley liked her
a lot, but it was a little hard to keep up with her sometimes.

Wembley and Mokey found Red near the big radish storage
bin. She was busily sorting through an enormous pile of lima
beans, her red pigtails bobbing as she worked. And as she worked,
she muttered to herself.

"Why should I have to deal with these dumb lima beans anyway?" Red muttered. "I mean, Boober is my friend and all, and
I like him well enough. But what's the point? Boober *hates* parties. Boober hates *everything!* Boy, this surprise party was a really
dumb idea. *Gobo's* dumb... humph!" She turned around and
noticed Mokey and Wembley.

"What do *you* want, Wembley?" Red said sourly.

"Gobo sent me to get you," Wembley said agreeably. "He
really needs those lima beans for the soup."

"Lima beans!" Red shouted. "Birthdays! Why did we have to
do all of this for old Boober, anyway?"

"Did I hear my name mentioned? Is something the matter?"
Boober's hat appeared around a corner, followed by his long
scarf. Boober always wore his hat and his scarf to protect him
from catching cold.

"Uh... Boober! Uh, hi! Uh, whatcha doing around here?"
Red said heartily.

"I came in for a snack. Why are you collecting all those lima
beans?" Boober looked nervous. "Are you hoarding them in
preparation for some kind of natural disaster?"

Red shook her head, exasperated. It was just like Boober to

go on about natural disasters! "No, Boober. I'm just...ah... doing a little favor for Gobo. Uh, isn't that right, Mokey?"

"Don't you worry, little Boober!" Mokey said cheerfully, putting her arm around him. "Remember, it's your birthday! No natural disaster would have the bad taste to happen on such a happy occasion!"

"For you it's a happy occasion," muttered Boober. "For me it's another year closer to the Great Abyss!"

"Oh, Boober. Don't be such a spoilsport!" Red exclaimed. "Boy, if you knew what we had been—"

"Knew what?" Boober asked, alarmed. "Knew what? Red, you'd better tell me! Is it something awful? I'm about to have a severe attack of hysterical panic!"

"So what else is new?" Red said glumly.

During all this time, Wembley had been making frantic signals at Mokey behind Boober's back. He pointed wildly toward the Hall, and made big soup-stirring movements with his hands. Then he pointed again, this time at the lima beans.

Unfortunately, Boober chose that moment to turn around. He looked at Wembley suspiciously. "You seem agitated, Wembley. What's wrong?"

"Agitated? No, I'm not agitated!" Wembley said agitatedly. "I'm just happy to see you! And Red! And Mokey! Especially Mokey!" Wembley pulled Mokey aside and began whispering frantically in her ear.

Boober watched them for a moment and then turned to Red. His voice shook. "It's bad news, Red. Something horrible has happened in Fraggle Rock. I can just *feel* it."

Red sighed. Here were Mokey and Wembley whispering secrets about Boober's silly party, and all Boober could think of was calamity and disaster. *"Boober,"* Red growled, "you are driving me *nuts!"*

At that moment Mokey and Wembley stopped whispering. "Red, I have a wonderful idea!" Mokey said sweetly.

"A wonderful idea!" Wembley echoed.

"Um...why don't you and Boober go on a...on a...on an adventure hike?" Mokey smiled radiantly.

"An adventure hike?" Boober stammered.

"An *adventure* hike? With *him?"* Red pointed to Boober.

"Yes!" Mokey was positively glowing. "To explore the beauties of the Spiral Cavern!"

"Me and Boober?" Red said. "In the Spiral Cavern? You've *got* to be kidding!"

Mokey gave Red a big wink. "I just *knew* you'd think it was a wonderful idea! Now, off you go." Mokey herded them gently out of the Pantry, leaning close to whisper in Red's ear as she passed. *"Keep him away from the Great Hall until party time."*

Red sighed and nodded. She turned to Boober, who looked puzzled but resigned. "Come on, Boober. Let's go have ourselves a laugh riot." And Red headed off briskly, with Boober trailing uncertainly behind her.

Mokey and Wembley watched their friends go. Then Mokey turned to the lima beans. "That should keep Boober away from the Great Hall," she said smugly.

"Do you think Boober caught on about the party?" Wembley asked.

"I don't think so, Wembley. Come on, now. We have to make some lima bean soup!"

2
The Spiral Cavern

THE Spiral Cavern was one of the strangest places in all of Fraggle Rock. It began with a huge circular ramp that wound down and down into a mysterious landscape filled with red and orange light. As Red led Boober around and down into the Cavern, she couldn't contain her excitement. "I just *love* it here!" she exclaimed.

Boober looked around mournfully as Red's words disappeared in tiny, perfect echoes. "Yes, indeed. The old downward spiral. Just what I need on my birthday."

Red ignored him, hopping toward the bottom of the ramp, where a narrow passage led into the darkness. "Hey, this looks interesting! Let's go this way!"

Boober peered into the gloomy tunnel. "Wh-what's down there?"

"How should I know?" Red shrugged. "That's what makes

this cavern so interesting!" And she headed down the path.

Boober didn't move. *He* wasn't going anywhere *near* that tunnel. All sorts of awful things probably lived there. And it looked damp and musty. He would catch pneumonia for sure, and that would be the end of *that.* No more birthdays for Boober.

Red had gotten halfway down the passage when she realized Boober wasn't behind her. She turned around to face him, her hands on her hips. "What are you worried about *now,* Boober?"

"I'm worried about the unknown and death and pain and spiders and words with *r* in them and…" Boober paused. "Do you want the whole list or just a general overview?"

Red shook her head in exasperation. "Have you ever noticed," she said, "that you and I have absolutely *nothing* in common?"

Boober sighed. "I worry about that, too."

Red rolled her eyes. "Look, it's your birthday, Boober. Let's just *pretend* we're having fun, okay?"

Boober nodded glumly, and they set off. They went down a set of stone steps and around a corner, and under an archway that was lower still. The arch led into a small, spooky space. Geysers puffed up steam from the floor and a single stalactite dripped water into a little puddle.

Red threw up her arms excitedly. "See, Boober? This is adventure! This is exciting!"

Boober looked around the tiny space and shuddered. "This is *terrifying!*"

"Hey, be a sport, huh? Let's go this way!" Red turned and marched even farther in.

Boober stayed where he was. He was *very* claustrophobic—confined spaces like this filled him with dread. As he looked cautiously around, Boober's eyes fell on a bright red sign that was fastened to the cave wall directly over Red's head. "Red, stop!" he whispered anxiously. "That's a falling rock zone!"

Red looked up at the warning sign and snorted. "That?" she exclaimed. "That's just for sissies. Come *on!*"

Red's voice echoed hugely in the little space. A rain of tiny pebbles fell from the ceiling. Red froze in her tracks and looked up in alarm. That did it for Boober. He completely panicked.

"There's going to be a cave-in, Red!"

Boober's voice triggered an avalanche of small rocks that bounced all around Red. Red was absolutely motionless. "Boober!" she whispered in alarm. "Don't! If you yell, you'll make it worse!"

But there was no stopping Boober now. He jumped up and down and wailed in total panic, *"We're going to die! We're going to die!"*

Somewhere nearby there was a deafening crash as an entire section of the cave's ceiling collapsed. With an expression of horror, Red dashed past Boober and back out toward the entrance to the Spiral Cavern. Boober was only steps behind her. They started to run back up the ramp, but it was too late. A gigantic circular boulder was rolling down the ramp toward them. Red and Boober screamed in terror and ran back in the opposite direction. The enormous boulder bounced down the ramp behind them. It was gaining ground.

And then there was too much dust to see anything.

Back in the Great Hall, no one had any way of knowing what had happened to Boober and Red. Gobo and Mokey were busily putting the finishing touches on the lima bean soup. Wembley stood around looking helpful.

"It's coming along nicely," Mokey said, stirring the broth with her wooden spoon. She took a tiny sip. "I think it needs a little more salt, though."

Gobo nodded energetically. "A little more salt? That's easy!" And he poured a big cup of salt into the soup.

Mokey took another sip. "Hmm. Now it needs a little *less* salt."

Gobo stared into the bubbling pot. "A little *less* salt? That will be harder."

Wembley bounced up and down beside his friend. "Hey, Gobo, how's it going?"

Gobo shook his head. "Well, we're just about ready for the party. Everyone's here but Red and Boober."

"Yeah," said Wembley. "They should be back by now."

"*Blaah-oooog! Blaah-oooog!*" Suddenly, the air was filled with the sound of the Fragglehorn! They all stopped what they were doing and looked around. What was happening?

Then a frantic Fraggle came running into the Great Hall, shouting at the top of his lungs. "CAVE-IN! THERE'S BEEN A CAVE-IN! DOWN BY THE SPIRAL CAVERN!"

Mokey turned as white as Boober's clean laundry. "Oh, no!" she cried. "That's where I sent Red and Boober!"

Gobo, Wembley, and Mokey looked at one another in horror. A cave-in in an underground world is about the worst thing that can happen. Around them, Fraggles were shouting and running around. The noise was deafening.

But Red and Boober, trapped behind the huge boulder in a tiny space at the base of the Spiral Cavern, could hear nothing at all.

3
Marooned!

"BOOBER? *Boober?* Are you okay?" Red's anxious voice rang out in the silence. The rock slide had stopped, and the dust was slowly settling.

"Ah-*choo!*" A sneeze rang out in the gloom. "Yes, I'm all right. For the moment. But it doesn't look good, does it?"

"Oh, Boober. Don't be such a pessimist! I've seen dozens of these old rock slides. All you do is push ... and shove ... and pull. You just use a little muscle. I'll have us out of here in no time!"

As she spoke, Red was pushing and shoving and pulling and using lots of muscle. But nothing seemed to be happening. The big boulder that had sealed them in wouldn't move.

Red paused for a moment and stood, panting. "The least you could do is help, Boober. Why should I have to do all the work around here?"

Boober shook his head sadly and pointed to the great boulder. "It's no use, Red," he said gloomily. "It would take a thousand Fraggles to move that rock."

"Nonsense! All it takes is...*umph*...is a little determination ...*umph*...and some elbow grease." Red continued to shove at the boulder.

"It won't do any good, Red," Boober sighed. "I'm afraid we're trapped...in this little tiny space."

Red looked around uneasily. "It is pretty small, isn't it? I can't take more than three steps in any direction." Red paced nervously around the little cave.

Boober nodded and sighed an even bigger sigh. "Yup, it's cozy, all right. Lucky for me that I have my claustrophobia under control. Otherwise, I'd feel like these walls were closing in on me...pressing in and in until—"

"Hey, Boober, quit it, would you?" Red's voice cracked slightly. "You're just making it worse."

"It would be hard to make it much worse than it is," Boober replied.

Red took a shaky breath. "Boy, Boober," she finally said with some of her usual energy, "you sure give up fast. I'll bet that right at this moment Gobo and Mokey and Wembley are coming to the rescue. After all," she went on, gathering confidence, "our friends would never give up on us. They'll figure out a way to save us."

This line of reasoning didn't impress Boober. "Remember who's head of the Rescue Squad? Felix the Fearless. He couldn't rescue a radish from a hungry Fraggle."

Red started to get a tight feeling in the pit of her stomach. "Our friends won't let anything happen to us," she said stubbornly. "Gobo will find us. He knows all the caves around here like the back of his hand."

"He may find us, all right," Boober said. "But once he does, what can he do? He'll never be able to dig us out. And we'll be stuck in this tiny little hole until we... until we..." Boober's voice trailed off.

"Stop it!" Red was beginning to feel very strange. Of course we'll get out! she thought angrily. It's just good old Boober again, making the worst of everything. Some Fraggle *he* is! Nothing's going to happen to *me!*

But something uneasy in the pit of Red's stomach kept rumbling. And Red Fraggle, the bravest of the brave, the best swimmer and diver and game player in all of Fraggle Rock, became aware of something awful.

She was beginning to be afraid.

When Felix the Fearless arrived on the scene, things had calmed down in the Great Hall. Felix was big by Fraggle standards, and *very* furry (all Fraggles are fairly furry). He wore a horned helmet and a heavy vest, and he carried thick coils of rope over both his shoulders. All in all, he looked like a Fraggle prepared for heroic deeds.

Felix stood on a ledge of rock high over the gathered crowd of Fraggles and looked down majestically. Then Mokey spotted him. "There he is!" she cried thankfully. "Felix the Fearless! Head of the Rescue Squad!"

"YAAAY!" shouted all the Fraggles. "Felix will save the day!"

Now that he had everyone's attention, Felix was in his element. He puffed out his chest, squared his shoulders, and felt very important. Then he paused dramatically. "Ah, what seems

to be the trouble?" he finally asked in a high-pitched voice.

"*Cave-in!*" a hundred Fraggle voices responded.

Felix frowned. "Oooh, I just *hate* those," he said. "Did anyone get...squashed?"

"Two of our friends are missing!" Gobo called up to him.

"Only you can save them!" Mokey cried.

"Come down and tell us what to do!" Wembley begged.

Now, that was just what Felix was waiting for! He had been practicing a special flying entrance for weeks now. He took one of his ropes, fashioned it into a lasso, twirled the loop high over his head, and tossed it over a distant crag of rock. He was ready!

With a loud "*halloo!*" he launched himself down toward the waiting Fraggles. Everything went perfectly until the end of his swing...when the rope broke. With an astonished gasp, Felix fell smack in the middle of the group of Fraggles...right on the seat of his pants.

"That's Felix," Gobo muttered to no one in particular. "Always landing on his feet."

The rest of the Fraggles ignored Felix's rather awkward entrance and gathered around him.

"Oh, Felix! We're so glad you're here!"

"We await your instructions!"

"Yaaay, Felix!"

Felix the Fearless stood up slowly and dusted off his trousers. Then he looked around at all the eager faces. They obviously expected him to do something dramatic and decisive. Felix bit his lip and thought hard. Then his face cleared.

"All right!" he said importantly. "I'm in command here. Listen hard and listen tight, because this is my first order. Okay ...uh...everyone line up in alphabetical order!"

Gobo sighed. Felix meant well, but he wasn't particularly good at organizing things—or at anything else, for that matter. While the Fraggles began milling around and sorting themselves into alphabetical order, Gobo moved toward Mokey. He leaned over and whispered in her ear, "This is hopeless, Mokey. I mean, I like Felix the Fearless as much as the next Fraggle, but the guy hasn't got a clue!"

Mokey nodded. "You're right, Gobo," she said. "But it's not really Felix's fault. After all, we've never had a major rescue before."

Gobo shook his head. "I know. But this isn't a practice session at a Fraggle picnic. This is for real! Those are our friends down there!"

"Shhh," whispered Mokey. "Give Felix a chance."

"Okay, okay." Gobo marched over and took his place in line as Felix reviewed the ranks of the assembled Fraggles.

Finally Felix cleared his throat loudly. "All right. First things first!" he announced. "We must locate the site of the cave-in."

"THE SPIRAL CAVERN!" shouted all the Fraggles.

Felix the Fearless nodded slowly. "Ah ... um ... in that case, we should go immediately to the Spiral Cavern! Follow me!"

Felix promptly marched off in the wrong direction.

"Excuse me, Felix." Gobo stepped out of line. "The Spiral Cavern is *this* way."

"Ah, right!" Felix said. "I was just turning around!" Felix

turned briskly and ran headfirst into Morris Fraggle. In the meantime Gobo had already started toward the Cavern.

Felix rubbed his head and pointed decisively at Gobo. "Follow him!" he shouted grandly.

And with Gobo leading the way, all the Fraggles marched off toward the Spiral Cavern. None of them knew what they would find, and all of them feared the worst. Would their rescue mission be too late? What had become of Red and Boober?

4

Fraggles to the Rescue

BACK in the Spiral Cavern, nothing much had changed. Red had tried to move the boulder, and then Boober had gotten up to help. They both pushed and pushed, but it wouldn't budge.

Red was sitting still now, her pigtails drooping dejectedly past her ears. Boober was still pushing away. She watched as he strained against the huge rock.

"I don't get it, Boober. I thought you said it was hopeless to try and move it," Red said.

"It's a...it's a...*total*...waste of time," gasped Boober. He paused to catch his breath. "But I know that we can't give up. Because if we give up...then..." Boober never finished his sentence. Both of them knew what he meant.

Red looked around the tiny space and then back at Boober. Somehow, the fact that he was actually trying to save them made their situation seem even worse. And deep inside, she realized she knew he was right. They could never move the boulder alone.

Never. The word sent chills down Red's back. They could *never* move the boulder. They would *never* get out of there. . . .

Red suddenly began to tremble. Then she started to take in big gulps of air. "I can't...breathe!" she gasped. And then Red totally lost control. She began sobbing wildly. *"I've got to get out of here! Please, somebody get me out of here!"*

Boober was stunned. He had never seen Red like this. He went over to her and grabbed her by the arm. "Red! Snap out of it! We have to cope!"

"I can't cope!" Red wailed. "I just want to go *home!*" Tears ran down her cheeks.

Boober took Red by the shoulders and shook her violently. "Come on, Red, calm down! If I can cope, *anybody* can cope!" Putting his arms around her, he began to rock her back and forth.

"I can't help it!" Red kept wailing. "We could die in here! I don't want to die in here!"

"Nobody wants to die," Boober said quietly. "That's why we have to help each other. We'll only make it worse if we're afraid."

Red sniffled, looking up at Boober with a puzzled expression on her face. "I don't understand," she said. "You're the one who's supposed to be terrified. I mean, you're *always* terrified. Of everything. I just don't get it."

"Neither do I," Boober replied. "But somehow, I'm not nearly as afraid as I used to be when I only *thought* that awful stuff was going to happen."

Red sniffled again, and a single tear ran down her cheek.

"Come on, Red," Boober continued. "You've always been the brave one."

Red shook her head sadly. She looked at Boober and then looked down at the ground. "A lot of the time I was really scared," she said softly. "Only I never let anybody see that."

"I never knew!" Boober exclaimed. "Why didn't you tell me before?"

Red shook her head and smiled a little smile. "I never told *anyone*. I'm supposed to be the brave one, silly."

Boober laughed. Then there was a long silence, broken only by the sound of their breathing.

"I m really glad you're here with me, Boober," Red said finally.

"It wouldn't be nice to be alone," Boober agreed. And he reached over and took Red's hand.

"What are we going to do now?" Red's voice shook.

Boober squeezed Red's hand and gave her a brave little smile. "Let's think about our friends and hope for the best. Only they can help us now."

As the rescue party of Fraggles headed down toward the Spiral Cavern, Gobo, Mokey, and Wembley were doing some serious thinking, too.

Gobo was out in front. He had a very determined look on his face. It was a look that inspired confidence. It was a look that said, "This is a Fraggle who can get his friends out of any trouble they might be in."

But deep inside, Gobo was worried. Were Red and Boober still okay? There was no way of telling. If they were, of course, Red was probably busy digging them out, with Boober moaning and groaning in the background. Love filled his heart as Gobo thought about his friends. That's exactly the way it would be—Red busily at work, and Boober busily worrying. It would be all right, Gobo decided, walking more quickly. It had to be.

Felix the Fearless was walking right next to Gobo. After all, as the official leader of the Rescue Squad, it was his duty to lead them all, even if he didn't know where he was going. In fact, since this was the first emergency Felix had ever had to deal with, not only did he not know where he was going but he had no idea what he was supposed to be doing. So he stuck his chin out and pushed ahead of Gobo. At least he would *look* like he was in control!

Mokey was following close behind. She kept trying to think positive thoughts about her friends. "They'll be fine. Red is always fine," she said to herself. But a nasty little voice kept intruding. *"It's your fault,"* the voice sneered. *"You sent them to the Spiral Cavern. If anything bad happens, you're to blame."*

Mokey shook her head to clear away the ugly voice. There was no point in feeling guilty. It certainly wouldn't help her friends. It was more important to send her positive thoughts out to Red and Boober: *"You'll be all right, Red and Boober. I know you will!"*

Wembley, who was right behind Mokey, was totally miserable. For once in his life he had stopped wembling (which is a Fragglish word that means "not being able to make up your mind"). Wembley had made up his mind. Things were awful.

Felix the Fearless was getting annoyed. They had been walking for *minutes,* and there was no sign of the cave-in. Maybe it was all a mistake. He was about to stop everyone and send them home for lunch when they turned a corner. Ahead of them was the great boulder that had sealed Red and Boober into their little hole. Rock dust still hung in the air.

Gobo stopped in his tracks when he saw the size of the boulder. "Oh, no," he said slowly. "It's worse than I thought."

Felix looked at him. "Is that the cave-in?" he asked. Gobo nodded gravely. Felix immediately whirled around to the other Fraggles. *"I've found the cave-in!"* he proclaimed importantly.

The crowd of Fraggles moved forward to look. Before anyone had a chance to say another word, Felix noticed the tip of Boober's scarf sticking out from under the great boulder. "Look at that! A scarf!"

Wembley and Mokey rushed forward.

"That's Boober's scarf!"

"Oh, no! What are we going to do?"

Felix shook his head gravely and looked around the crowd. "Looks to me as if your friends are already squashed. It's hopeless. Let's go get some lunch." Felix took a step, but Gobo moved to block his path.

"Hey, wait a minute," Gobo cried. "I happen to know that there was a little cave where that boulder is now! Maybe they're still alive. We can't just give up!"

Felix shrugged. "Be my guest. Maybe *you've* got a brilliant idea for moving that boulder."

Gobo turned to the crowd. "All I know is we gotta try! Come on, everybody!"

A moment later Fraggles were all over the boulder, shoving and pushing for all they were worth. Not surprisingly, it didn't move an inch.

"See what I mean?" said Felix. "We're never going to get them out of there. Let's go eat."

That was it for Gobo. He'd heard enough of Felix's nonsense. "Felix, if you can't contribute, just stand aside, okay?"

"B-but ... I'm the head of the Rescue Squad!" stammered Felix.

Gobo stood his ground. "Look, Felix, those are our friends in there. And we're not giving up." Gobo turned to Mokey. "Mokey, start tying those ropes together, okay? We'll have to make a harness that we can tie to the boulder. And let's get moving. We have some hard work ahead of us."

Felix mumbled and grumbled, but he finally decided it would be better to stay out of the way. He couldn't figure out anything to do—which must mean that there was nothing *to* do. If things turned out badly, no one could blame him. After all, he had warned them.

While Mokey and a group of Fraggles were busy with the rock harness, Wembley moved toward Gobo. Wembley had never seen his friend this serious, even when Gobo was embarking on a perilous adventure.

"How does it look to you, Gobo?" he asked.

Gobo looked grave. "We just have to try," he said finally. "But we had better be ready for anything."

Wembley gulped. "Wh-what do you mean?"

Gobo looked straight into Wembley's eyes. "I mean ... this might not have a happy ending."

5

Is This the End?

On the other side of the great boulder, Red and Boober knew nothing of the rescue attempt. They were sealed in so tightly that they couldn't hear a thing.

They had long ago stopped trying to dig their way out. Now they were sitting in silence on opposite sides of the cramped chamber, thinking their own private thoughts.

Red spoke first. "You know, Boober, there's something I've always wanted to ask you," she said, looking over at her friend. "Fraggle Rock is such a fun place! There's lots of great stuff to do...but you were always so unhappy. I just don't get it."

Boober thought for a moment. "I guess maybe I never really believed in being happy. It was too risky. I always had this feeling that the good stuff would never last long enough. And if stuff was going to disappoint me anyway, I might as well be prepared and stay a little disappointed all the time."

Red looked at Boober in astonishment for a second and then burst out laughing. "But that's so *dumb!* I mean, then you're always disappointed."

"Not *really* disappointed," Boober said a little huffily. "Just *semi*-disappointed."

"Oh, Boober." Red came over and sat beside him. "You know what I think?"

"What?" Boober asked.

"I think you're really weird." Red paused and patted Boober's arm. "And...really neat."

Boober swallowed hard and blinked at Red. When he spoke, his voice shook just a little. "Nobody ever told me I was neat before. Especially not you, Red. You always acted so angry at me all the time."

It was Red's turn to think for a moment. "I guess I *was* mad at you, Boober. Just a little bit, anyway. I was always planning great things, and you were always talking about how they wouldn't turn out. It got really depressing sometimes."

"I see what you mean." Boober nodded. "I guess no one wants to listen to someone who keeps telling them that everything is going to be terrible."

Red shook her head. "No, Boober. That's just not fair. You have a right to feel any way you do. Even if you *are* wrong." And Red laughed a little at her joke.

Boober smiled. "That reminds me of a joke I once heard," he said.

Red looked at him in amazement. *"You* know *jokes?"* she asked.

Boober blushed. "Don't tell anyone, okay? But whenever I heard a good one, I used to write it on a little piece of paper and stick it somewhere secret—at the bottom of a drawer or in the toe of an old sock. Some of them are even funny. Want to hear a great laundry joke?"

"Sure," Red said.

"Okay. Um, you know, laundry can be very dangerous to do, Red."

"Dangerous?" Red asked. "How?"

"Uh, haven't you ever gotten a sock on the nose?"

Red smiled and shook her head. "Oh, Boober, that was *silly.*"

"I know," Boober shrugged. "Want to hear some more?"

So Boober told Red all his favorite laundry jokes, and then Red did her favorite impersonations—the ones she usually saved for parties. She imitated the way Gobo talked about all his great adventures, and the way Mokey read her poetry, and the way Wembley got all flustered and confused when he was wembling.

At the end of her impersonations, they were both breathless with laughter.

"That was really great, Red," gasped Boober. "For a moment, it was almost like having Gobo, Mokey, and Wembley here with us."

"Yeah," Red said softly. "It makes me feel really good just to think about them." She looked around the tiny space. "Well, Boober," she said finally, "you've told all your jokes. I've done all my impersonations. Now what?"

"Let's keep concentrating on our friends," Boober whispered. "I don't know why, but just *thinking* about them makes me feel stronger."

Outside of Red and Boober's hole, Gobo and Mokey had finished hooking up the rock harness. Gobo adjusted the ropes,

which were fixed to rings and hooks and pulleys. It looked very impressive.

"That ought to do it," he said finally, standing back to admire his handiwork. He looked behind him. A long line of Fraggles stretched out of the passage, holding the rope. There were at least fifty of them involved in the rescue operation.

Wembley watched as Gobo made the final adjustments to the harness. "I'm sure glad you know how to do this, Gobo," he said, proud of his best friend.

That made Gobo smile. "I've never seen a rock harness before in my life, Wembley," Gobo said wistfully. "I just sort of made it up. I don't know if it will work."

"B-but...it *has* to work, Gobo!"

"I know," Gobo said quietly. He paused and looked back at the great boulder. "Sooner or later they'll run out of air in there."

Gobo and Wembley stared at one another for a long moment. Then Gobo turned to the waiting Fraggles.

"Ready?" Gobo called.

"READY!" the Fraggles shouted back.

"Okay!" Gobo yelled. "On the count of three! One! Two! *Three!*" And the Fraggles began to sway and chant in unison, pulling with all their might at the ropes in their hands.

"*Rock, rock, rock... heave! Rock, rock, rock... heave!*" The Fraggles rocked and heaved for all they were worth. As the chant continued, Gobo raced up and down the line, encouraging them to greater and greater effort. "Dig in your heels!" he cried. "Do it together. Give it everything you've got!"

"*Rock, rock, rock...heave!*" The Fraggles strained even harder against the ropes.

Felix the Fearless stood to the side, watching the Fraggles

work. They'll never do it, he thought. And then the boulder moved! *"It's moving! It's moving!"* he screeched.

"Rock, rock, rock . . . heave!"

"Heave! Heave!" shouted Gobo. "It's starting to move!"

The Fraggles heaved with all their might.

Suddenly, thick clouds of rock dust billowed out from the ceiling of the Cavern. Then an ominous rumbling was heard, followed by a rain of little rocks. Felix was the first to panic. "Run!" he screamed. "Run for your lives! The whole place is caving in!" And a herd of terrified Fraggles followed him as he dashed for the ramp of the Spiral Cavern.

Only Gobo, Wembley, and Mokey stood their ground, holding each other's hands. "We can't leave. Our friends need us," Mokey said. The noise was so loud that Gobo and Wembley could barely hear her. But they knew what she was saying. And all three bravely waited for whatever would happen next.

Inside Red and Boober's hole, the movement of the boulder had made things even worse. First there was a rain of fist-sized boulders from the ceiling. Red and Boober screamed in panic and tried to protect their heads with their hands.

"No! No! Somebody help us!"

"We're going to die!"

Then, as the cave rumbled and shook, the ceiling suddenly dropped straight down toward them! Red and Boober fell to the ground in terror. This was it! The end! The whole ceiling would collapse and they would be crushed! There was barely time to think of anything before . . . suddenly . . . everything grew quiet.

When the dust cleared, Red and Boober discovered that there was only enough room left in the cave for them to sit side by side. The roof of their little prison was now only a few feet above their heads, and fallen rocks had filled most of the other space.

"I think I'm still alive," Red whispered.

"Me, too," murmured Boober.

There was a long, long pause. Red and Boober just breathed and sat very still in the tiny space that was left. There was no point in doing or saying anything now. From the very beginning, they had been in desperate trouble. Now the situation looked worse. There wasn't even room to turn around. They were trapped where they sat, perhaps forever. The silence stretched on and on as Red and Boober thought about this.

Finally, after what seemed like hours, Boober turned toward Red and said, "It's very quiet now. Maybe they've stopped trying to rescue us."

Red nodded. "Yeah. Maybe."

There was another long pause. Then Red said, "You know, Boober, I feel kind of giddy."

"Yeah, giddy and tired," Boober replied. "You know what that means, don't you?"

"It means we're running out of air," Red said simply.

Boober nodded sadly. There was another long pause as the horrible truth began to sink in. Then Red said almost cheerfully, "What do you think it's like to die?"

"I can't imagine what it's like," Boober said. "I don't think anybody can."

Red blinked back a tear. "But when you think about death, what do you think?"

Boober sighed. "Well, the way I see it, being born is on one end...and dying is on the other...and in between there's this...." Boober's voice trailed away into silence.

"Keep going," Red said. "I'm listening."

Boober took a ragged breath. "You know, I remember this one day I was doing my laundry and this big soap bubble floated up from the tub . . . and there it was in front of my face, so beautiful and shiny, and then . . ."—Boober let out a long sigh and gulped back a tear—"and then . . . it was *gone.*" Boober said the word *gone* as if he could hardly believe it.

Red gave a sniffle. She was starting to cry again.

"Don't be sad," Boober whispered.

"I can't help it," Red whimpered. "I want life to stay."

"We all do, Red. Look at it this way. We were lucky to have been a part of it . . . all the good times and laughs and songs and stuff."

Red gave a little laugh. "You always said you hated good times and laughs and songs."

Boober cleared his throat and said in a tiny voice, "Well, sometimes I liked them. But that's a secret."

Red gave Boober a little hug. "Aw, Boober, your tail is wagging."

"Stupid tail," Boober said. "It always did give me away."

There was another long pause.

"Don't go to sleep, Red, okay?"

Red nodded wordlessly. She knew what Boober meant. They were running out of air. If they went to sleep, they might not wake up again.

6
Saved!

When things had settled down on the other side of the boulder, the Fraggles—all except Felix, who had gone to lunch—began creeping slowly down the ramp of the Spiral Cavern to see what damage had been done. All of them feared that Gobo, Mokey, and Wembley had met the same fate as Red and Boober.

But when they reached the bottom of the Cavern, they could see the three Fraggles, still standing in the dust and rubble. "They're okay," yelled someone, and the cry was passed back along the Fraggle lines. Slowly a crowd began to gather.

"What are we going to do, Gobo?"

"Felix says we should give up. It's too dangerous down here."

"What do you think, Gobo?"

Gobo cleared his throat, and the murmuring Fraggles fell silent. "All I know is," he said solemnly, "that they're going to run out of air down there if we don't do something." His voice rose slightly. "I'm not giving up without a fight. Who's with me?"

"I am, Gobo."

"Me, too."

"I'm with you, Gobo!"

Gobo slowly smiled. "So let's move that rock!"

The rock harness was again hooked up to the boulder and the Fraggles took their positions. For a moment they stood in silence. As they did, the ceiling rock above their heads gave a great groan. They looked up anxiously. Would it come crashing down on their heads as soon as they began heaving on the great boulder?

Gobo hopped up on a ledge, and a hundred Fraggle eyes turned toward him. "Okay, we haven't got much time! I want you all with me on the count of three—*one...two...three!*"

"Rock, rock, rock...heave! Rock, rock, rock...heave!"

The Fraggles threw themselves against the rock harness with all their might. But the great boulder did not move.

"Harder!" Gobo shouted. "Harder!"

All was silent on the other side of the great boulder. Red and Boober had fallen asleep.

"Rock, rock, rock...heave!"

The great boulder shifted slightly, and the ceiling began to rumble, louder this time.

"Don't stop!" shouted Gobo. "It's starting to move!"

The Fraggles pulled and pulled on the rock harness as the first large boulders came down from the ceiling and landed with huge thuds.

"Ignore them!" Gobo cried. "It's rolling!"

And rolling it was, inch by inch.

"We've broken through!" Gobo screamed. "PULL!"

The boulder moved another inch, and rocks rubbed against each other with a sound like thunder. Gobo scrambled to look through the narrow opening into Red and Boober's cave. Wembley was at his side.

"Are they alive?" Wembley cried.

"I don't know! I can't see yet!" Gobo raised his voice. "Red! Boober! Are you in there?"

Red and Boober lay in the tiny space, motionless. Gobo pushed partway into the chamber. The dust settled slightly. And then he could make out the bodies of his friends, lying on the cave floor. Gobo's heart stopped. Were they...were they...

But, as if awakening from a dream, Boober stirred slightly. He sat up slowly and looked around.

"Come on, Boober! Get Red! This whole place is going to cave in!"

Boober shook his head and suddenly realized where he was. He grabbed Red by the shoulders. "Red! Wake up!" Red made a little noise and rolled over. "Red!" Boober said urgently. "We've got to get out of here! *Wake up!*"

Finally Red opened her eyes and looked up in confusion. "Come on, Red," Boober said. "It's time to go home." Boober took Red's hand, and they crawled toward the crack in the wall that led to freedom. Gobo waited for them on the other side and helped pull them both through to safety. Red and Boober weren't a half step out of the hole when the entire ceiling fell in behind them with a huge crash, sending up showers of boulders and billowing dust.

"Let's get out of here!" Gobo yelled. "This whole place could come down at any moment!"

All the Fraggles fled up the ramp of the Spiral Cavern. Gobo was the last to leave. When he reached the top, Red and Boober were standing unsteadily in a large circle of Fraggles. Mokey and Wembley were hugging them both.

Gobo slowly smiled a big smile. "Come on, you guys. There's a party waiting!"

Boober's surprise birthday party was one of the greatest Fraggle celebrations in the history of Fraggle Rock. There was singing and dancing and playing and laughing and a zillion other things to bring joy to any Fraggle heart. And the happiest Fraggle hearts in the room belonged to our five Fraggle friends.

Boober and Red were sitting in the place of honor in the center of the Great Hall. Their friends were gathered around them.

"It must have been terrible down there. Boy, am I glad you're okay!" Gobo grinned happily.

"Me, too!" Wembley chimed in.

"I just *knew* everything would turn out all right," Mokey said. "We all love you so much...nothing bad could have happened to you!"

Red and Boober just smiled and smiled.

"Come on, you guys," Gobo proclaimed, "let's get our guests of honor some refreshments! Felix, let's have some lima bean soup and sparkling radish juice here!"

"*Felix?*" Wembley laughed.

"Uh-huh," Gobo said, smiling. "Felix has a new job—official Fraggle chef, third class! He was always so interested in having lunch that he decided that food was his true vocation. Now, instead of stirring up trouble, he's stirring up the soup!"

"Well, it may be a new job, but it looks as if he still needs some help," Mokey said. "Let's go get something to eat!"

The three friends rushed off, leaving Boober and Red alone.

Boober and Red looked at one another for one long, joyous minute. Then Boober leaned close to Red and whispered in her ear. "Ah...um...Red...you know that business about me liking songs and games?"

Red smiled shyly. "And that stuff about me being afraid?"

Boober moved closer. "Those are our secrets, right?"

"Right!" Red said happily, giving Boober a little squeeze. "We'll never tell anyone about any of it!"

And they never did.